KAREN LYNN WILLIAMS

Baseball and Butterflies

ILLUSTRATED BY LINDA STORM

Lothrop, Lee & Shepard Books
New York

First Edition 1 2 3 4 5 6 7 8 9 10

Library of Congress Cataloging in Publication Data
Williams, Karen Lynn.
Baseball & butterflies / by Karen Lynn Williams ; illustrated by Linda Storm.
    p.   cm.   Summary: At the end of the third grade, Daniel finds his summer
butterfly project threatened by his bratty little brother and his friends' obsession
with baseball.   ISBN 0-688-09489-9   [1. Brothers—Fiction.   2. Butterflies—
Fiction.   3. Baseball—Fiction.]   I. Storm, Linda, ill.   II. Title.   III. Title: Baseball and butterflies.   PZ7.W66655Bas   1990   [Fic]—dc20   90-5713   CIP   AC

For Steven

1

"Your move, bonehead," Daniel groaned. "Let's get this game over with."

"It is not," Joey yelled. "I just moved." Daniel and Joey were playing Stratego on the front porch. Joey picked up one of the blue pieces and slammed it down again, nearly upsetting the game board. "And don't call me bonehead. Mom," he yelled. "Daniel's teasing again."

"I don't play with tattletales," Daniel warned his younger brother. He sighed and moved a red captain one space forward. "My six takes your eight," he said, tossing the blue piece into his pile.

"I am not a tattletale. Mo-o-om, Daniel's calling me names," Joey called through the screen door.

Daniel had to laugh. Joey had a real temper for such a little guy. You wouldn't know it to look at him, with all that straight blond hair hanging into his eyes and that little round nose. People were always stopping them, even strangers, ooing and ahhing. "Sooo cute!" they always said. Then they'd say, "Are you two brothers?" reminding Daniel of his own curly hair and freckles. Yuck! "Curly Girly," the kids used to call him in second grade. Daniel had hated it.

Normally, Daniel thought, he'd have refused to play with Joey at all. Joey was always begging to play and then mixing up the moves. And he was always tattling. But today was different. It was the first day of summer vacation. Third grade was over for good. No more homework. No more spelling. And no more grief from Mom about how messy his handwriting was and how neat Joey's was. "Look at your brother's work and he's only in first grade." He could still hear it.

Nope, Daniel thought. Don't have to think about any of that for the whole summer. No

school, the pool was open, and Eddie's birthday party was on Friday. He stretched out on his stomach on the mat on the front porch and took a deep breath. The air smelled sweet and clean. This would be a great summer. The best.

"Butterfly," Joey yelled as he jumped up, knocking over all the pieces. "Monarch."

"Get the nets," Daniel directed his brother. "I'll watch it." Joey was already through the front door.

"Should have had those nets out here," Daniel muttered to himself. He raced down the steps, keeping his eye on the beautiful black and orange insect as it glided effortlessly, first up to the treetops and then down to the dandelions. I could use a new monarch for my collection, Daniel thought.

"Here." Joey stuck a net in front of Daniel and kept running.

Daniel made a few swishing arcs in the air. It felt good and he was off after his brother. "Hey, that's mine," he said. "Out of the way, Joey." Joey was always in the way, into everything that Daniel tried to do.

"I saw it first," Joey called.

"You'll lose him," Daniel warned as Joey took

a couple of swipes at the insect that was way over his head.

The butterfly doubled back toward Daniel. Too high. In a second, it had gone behind Mrs. Berger's house. By the time Daniel reached the corner, it was out of sight.

"Gone," Joey said.

"Yeah, you should have stayed with it," Daniel told him. "You're always bragging about how fast you can run."

"I'm the one who had to get the nets," Joey reminded his brother.

Oh well, Daniel thought. Who cares? What's one butterfly? Today was the first day of summer. There would be hundreds of butterflies— monarchs, admirals, swallowtails, maybe even a luna moth this year. The warm sidewalk felt good on his bare feet.

"It's going to be a great summer," he said out loud to no one. He waved his net through the air and thought about the endless number of sunny days that lay before him.

2

Daniel's desk was cluttered with leftover school papers and rocks from his rock collection. There were several pieces of shiny coal and an almost fossilized cow's tooth. He put the box that held his butterfly collection down on top of it all. It was a neat box with glass doors. His mom had bought it at a garage sale.

"Those butterflies look a little messy. What happened?" Joey asked.

"Who asked you?" Daniel said, brushing out the pieces of wings that had fallen to the bottom of the case. They crumbled into nothing when he touched them. Butterfly wings were so light, lighter than paper, than air almost, and so beautiful. Daniel felt bad that some of them were spoiled.

"Have you been into my collection?" he asked Joey.

"Not me," Joey said, looking cross-eyed at a strand of his own hair.

"I bet you did."

"No I didn't."

"Liar."

"I'll tell Mom you called me a liar."

"Forget it," Daniel said. "I'm making a new collection anyway."

"Hey, it could be both of ours. I could make the labels—neatly." Joey emphasized the last word.

"Beat it," Daniel told Joey. "Can't a guy have a little peace in his own room?"

"I caught some of those butterflies."

"You can't even tell a monarch from a fritillary. It's my collection, so scram."

"This is my room too." Joey folded his arms across his chest.

"No kidding." Daniel said, eyeing the sports posters all over Joey's half of the room. The newest one was football. The guy looked like an ape.

"I was here first," Daniel said. He hated sharing his room with a brat.

"Mo-o-om. Daniel says I can't stay in my own room."

"Boys, stop that arguing," Mom's voice called from the stairway. "Now."

Dad came to the bedroom door. "I'm on my way back to the office, boys. Take it easy. It's going to be a hot one. Joey, why don't you come down and practice on your bike. Give Daniel a break." Joey made a face at his brother and went downstairs with his dad.

"Bye, Dad. Thanks," Daniel called after them.

Daniel looked at his butterflies again. Somehow, they didn't look quite the same pinned onto brown cardboard as they did against the blue sky. Maybe I'll try a white background, he thought. I could even use shiny foil or something. Too bad they have to be pinned.

"Disgusting," Molly Brenden had said right out loud in front of the whole class when he'd brought the butterflies to school last year. "That's unhumane. You should be reported to the Humane Society, Daniel King." Molly's father was a policeman. She was always reporting someone to something.

What did she know? That's the way they did it at the museum. Daniel had taken a class there, and he had learned the proper way to prepare samples for a collection.

If only there was a better way to keep them so they would stay beautiful, Daniel thought.

"Hey, Dan, want to play some baseball down at Eddie's?" It was his best friend, Brian, from around the corner.

"Your mom said you were up here," Brian said, looking over Daniel's shoulder. "Looks like you need some new butterflies," he added, eyeing the powdered wings.

"Yeah," Daniel agreed. "Want to help me catch some?"

"Maybe later," Brian said. "Right now everyone's at Eddie's waiting to play ball."

Daniel sighed. He wasn't very good at baseball. Last summer he'd been the only second grader who was still a half out. He didn't care for the game much. He was usually last to be picked for a team and last up at bat. All he ever got to do was stand in the outfield.

"I don't know," Daniel said. "It's kind of hot."

"Oh, come on. It's early. We need more players. If you play, I'll help catch butterflies later. You can be a whole out this year too."

"OK, for a while. I'll get my mitt. Meet you outside." Daniel stuffed his bare feet into his sneakers without bothering to tie them and ran downstairs.

He wheeled his bike out of the garage and walked it down the driveway to the sidewalk, where Brian was waiting on his bike.

"Hey, wait for me." Daniel looked over his shoulder and saw Joey balancing his bike against the curb. He used the curb for a step to get on his bike. His glove was hanging from the handlebars.

"You can't come," Daniel called to his brother. "We're going to Eddie's."

"I sure can, and you can't stop me. Summer of first grade, remember?"

The summer of first grade! That's when Joey had been promised he could go around the block by himself. Daniel had forgotten. Joey had been practicing on his two-wheeler for this chance all spring.

Figures, Daniel thought. Of course he'd had to wait until second grade to ride around the block. But Joey got to do everything earlier. He'd even

14

started getting an allowance one whole year younger than Daniel had. Joey lost his first tooth early too. Just six days after Daniel had lost his first tooth, Joey lost his. And one week later, he lost another. It wasn't fair.

"I guess we're stuck," he told Brian.

"That's OK," Brian said. "We need more kids. He can be half out." Brian pushed off up the hill.

"Hey, wait up," Daniel called as he slid his mitt over his handlebars. He pumped up the hill as fast as he could to keep ahead of Joey.

Great! Daniel thought. Not only was everyone into baseball again this summer, but this year his baby brother had to tag along.

3

Daniel hopped off his bike in Eddie's driveway and let it fall on the grass. Ian, Reed, Greg, and Catherine were already in the backyard, playing. Molly was at bat. Everyone called Molly a "slugger." She was skinny but she could sure slam that ball. Daniel headed for the outfield.

"Hey, Curly Girly," someone called. Eddie's older brother, Tom, was sitting in the grass. "See you got yourself a baby to sit," he added as Joey came around the corner of the house and followed his brother to the outfield.

Daniel blushed. He hated that Tom Cole. When Tom had started middle school last year,

Daniel thought his troubles were over. You were OK if Tom didn't notice you, but if he decided to pick on you there was nothing you could do. Daniel remembered two years ago when Tom used to tease Molly's older sister every day on the way home from school just because she had red hair. Sara had to find a new route home.

Now it looked like Tom would be around for the summer. One more thing to spoil Daniel's vacation.

"Let's play ball," Brian called. "You want to play, Tom?"

"I don't play with babies," Tom said. "I'll just watch and see you don't make mistakes."

I'll bet, Daniel thought.

Eddie pitched the ball to Molly. Before Daniel could get ready, she had smacked it over the fence.

"Way to go, slugger," Greg yelled.

"Hey, Daniel," Eddie called, "you or Joey should have had that. Now we've already lost the ball."

"I see it," Daniel said. He carefully moved the prickers off the back fence and climbed over. He knew he shouldn't have come. He'd probably never even get his ups. Maybe he should just go home.

Daniel tossed the ball back over the fence. Joey caught it and threw it straight to Eddie. "Whoa," Tom called from the side. "Little kid's got a pretty good arm."

Brian hit a ground ball to first base before Daniel even got back over the fence. Joey was already there to catch it and tagged Brian out. "Not bad," Ian said. Brian and Eddie were impressed too.

Daniel moved, in for the next hitter. "Hey, Daniel, get back out there," Eddie called.

Boring, Daniel thought as he watched a few more plays. "How about letting me pitch?" he called to Eddie.

"No way," Eddie said. "This is my yard."

"You couldn't even get it over the plate, Curly," Tom added.

Daniel sighed. He'd like to clobber that Tom Cole, but he knew he never would.

It was getting hotter. His feet were sweaty. Maybe they'd go to the pool that afternoon or take their nets to the park, maybe catch some . . . A swallowtail, right there on Eddie's mom's flowers! It was resting its golden wings, opening and closing them like fans. Daniel dropped his mitt and started to tiptoe toward the flower bed. He held his breath and slowly inched his hand forward.

Thump. The ball landed on the ground next to him. Daniel blinked, and the butterfly was gone.

"Daniel!" Eddie yelled. "That would have been the third out!"

"He was just trying to catch a butterfly," Joey yelled back. "Look, there it goes, a monarch."

"A swallowtail," Daniel hissed at Joey.

"That's great. I don't believe it," crowed Tom. "Wait until I tell the guys this one. Curly Girly chases butterflies in the outfield." He was rolling on the ground laughing.

Thinks he's a hyena, Daniel thought. His face was hot with embarrassment. "Big mouth," Daniel said, glaring at Joey.

"Joey gets last ups," Eddie said when their team was finally up. "And you're next to last," he told Daniel.

That's something, Daniel figured. With Joey around at least he wasn't dead last anymore. Maybe he'd get up after all, although he wasn't

sure he wanted to be up at bat with Tom making all those comments.

Eddie was up first because it was his yard. He was good too, Daniel had to admit. He hit the ball over Brian's head and made it to third base. Catherine was up next. She made it to first and Eddie came home. One run. Daniel sat in the shade and waited for his ups.

Joey was jumping around near the first-base line, cheering the runners. "Run," he called to Catherine before Ian even hit the ball. Then Ian hit a fly ball. Brian caught it and tagged Catherine out before she got back to first base.

"That's two outs. Who's up?" Eddie called.

"Daniel. Hey, Daniel's up," Tom called. "Keep your eye on the ball. Any swing at a butterfly is an out."

Daniel picked up a bat and stood at home plate. He wished Tom would go away. One more out and he'd probably make it, Daniel thought as he waited for the pitch. That made him nervous. He swung too soon. Strike. Daniel choked up on the bat. This time the pitch almost hit him. He jumped back and swung. "Strike two," Brian called.

"Should have let it go," Eddie told Daniel.

One more shot, Daniel thought. Maybe just once he'd hit that ball like Molly did, send it flying like it had wings.

"Daniel swings like he's afraid of the ball," Tom called. "He's scared."

Thwack. Daniel hit the ball off the tip of the bat. It rolled over toward the first-base line. Foul, he thought and stood there.

"Run, Daniel," Joey called. "You hit it."

Greg scooped up the ball and tapped Daniel on the arm.

"Out," called Brian. "We're up."

"Finally hits the ball and forgets to run," Tom said.

"I don't even get my ups," Joey moaned.

"Clam up," Daniel warned his brother.

"Wait a minute," Eddie called. "It's only a half out. Joey still gets his ups."

"I promised Daniel he'd be a whole out," Brian said.

"Well, I didn't say he could," Eddie protested.

"Oh, come on, Eddie, just because you're losing."

"It's his yard," Tom called from the sidelines. Daniel wished he could disappear.

"That's right," Eddie agreed. Eddie always acted tough when his brother was around.

"Forget it," Daniel said. "I quit anyway." His face felt hot from the inside and his eyes were watery. He walked down the driveway and picked up his bike.

"Where're you going?" Joey called.

Daniel didn't answer. He rode down the sidewalk. The breeze felt good.

The problem was, Tom was right, Daniel thought. Partly right, anyway. He *was* afraid of the ball. It was a hard ball and Brian really threw it. Mostly, though, he didn't care enough about the game, at least not enough to get hit with the ball or to stay and listen to Tom Cole. He had better things to do.

4

There are more than six hundred species of swallowtails worldwide, Daniel read. The carpet smelled like perfume. It gave him a headache. Daniel rolled over on his back. *Their eggs are round, and the caterpillar has prominent eyespots.*

That's it, Daniel thought. Wonder how I could get some eggs, raise caterpillars, make a kind of butterfly farm.

The screen door slammed. "Where's Daniel?" he heard Joey ask Mom. Quickly, Daniel rolled over and slid his book under his bed. Next thing, the blabbermouth would be telling the whole world that Daniel was spending summer vacation reading, like some kind of weirdo.

"Hey, Daniel," Joey announced from the doorway. "I hit a double after you left. They said I could play tomorrow. Maybe by the end of the summer I'll be a whole out."

"So what?" Daniel muttered. Great, he thought. Even his baby brother played baseball better than he did.

"Hey, what's Eddie's new book doing under the bed?"

"That's my book," Daniel said, "and you leave it alone."

"Well, Mom got one just like it for Eddie's birthday. A butterfly book."

"You're lying."

"I am not. Mom," Joey called, heading out of the room, "Daniel says I'm a liar."

"Mo-om." Daniel called, pushing ahead of Joey on the stairs. "Did you get a *book* for me to take to Eddie's party?" He went through the kitchen to the laundry room.

"Two books," said Mom. "That butterfly one you like so much and the mystery with the rabbit on the cover."

26

"Mom, I can't take a book to a birthday party," Daniel pleaded. "No way."

"Listen, Daniel." Mom stopped folding the clothes. "As long as I pay for the birthday presents around here, they will be things I feel are worth spending my money on."

"But, Mom, no one brings books." The kids would laugh him right out of the party, Daniel thought. And Eddie doesn't even read.

"No arguing."

Plop. Plop. Plunk. Two nickles and a quarter fell onto Daniel's bed as he shook his bank. He reached around inside the hole with his finger and pulled out a dollar bill. It almost tore. Daniel stretched his finger in the hole as far as it would go and felt all the way around. Then he closed one eye and put the other one up to the hole. Empty. One dollar and thirty-five cents. That wasn't enough to buy Eddie a decent gift.

Books. That was worse than, than . . . than underwear. Daniel remembered the time Martin Howard brought Ian a set of He Man underwear as a birthday present. Undershirt, pants, and socks. Everyone at the party chased Martin around with the underwear, yelling "Cooties," and Martin wasn't invited to another party for two years.

This summer was turning out to be awful. His butterfly collection was ruined. His baby brother followed him everywhere. And now he had to bring books to Eddie's party. Maybe I'll just stay in bed with the covers over my head, Daniel thought, for the whole summer.

5

On Tuesday, Daniel stood in front of the bathroom mirror and pulled a curl from the top of his head, straight down. It reached the end of his nose. He stuck his tongue up and wondered if he could grab the hair with his teeth. Too short.

Crooked teeth, Daniel thought. His two front teeth were huge, and one slanted in front of the other. It made a little cave for his tongue to explore. Joey's teeth were perfect, straight and neat like his handwriting. "Daniel's going to need braces," Mom kept saying. "That will cost a lot of money," she kept telling Daniel, as if it was his fault. Daniel stuck his tongue in the cave. He wondered if braces hurt. Daniel couldn't stand Joey and his straight teeth and his straight hair and his neat handwriting.

He slopped some water on his head with the washcloth. It splashed the mirror and dripped onto the floor. He combed the curls down flat.

"Butterfly alert." Daniel heard Joey run through the downstairs to the back hall where the nets were. "Whirrrr, whirrr. Butterfly alert."

Why does he have to act so dumb? Daniel wondered as he ran down the stairs. Like it's some kind of a game. He sure is great at spotting butterflies, though.

"It's huge," Joey called to him. "A real beauty, black and yellow tiger stripes."

Swallowtail, Daniel thought as he ran out the front door. Perfect for his new breeding project. "Get a jar and the hammer and nails from Mom," he called to Joey. "I'll get this one."

The butterfly seemed to speed up as Daniel ran closer to it. He knows I'm after him, he thought. It's amazing how they know. The butterfly flew jerkily up and down but suddenly circled back toward Daniel. Daniel stopped and waited patiently. The butterfly almost landed. Swish. "Got him."

"Aren't you going to kill it? Pin it down?" Joey asked as he watched his brother put the net down with a twist so the butterfly couldn't escape. It lay quietly trapped in the netting.

"Not this time," Daniel explained as he pounded holes in the top of the jar with a nail. "I'm going to try to mate it. Just have to find out if this one is a male or female."

"What are the holes for?" Joey asked.

Daniel sighed. "Don't you know anything? For air. Now get some grass and a small stick for the jar."

Daniel gently released the butterfly into the jar and clapped the top on. He'd have to get some water in there somehow and . . . He looked over the porch railing at Mom's garden. "Get one of those yellow flowers," he told Joey.

"Not me," Joey said. "Mom says no picking flowers."

Daniel sighed and ran down the steps. He snipped off a marigold and carefully dropped it into the jar with the grass and the stick and the butterfly.

"I'm telling," Joey said. "You picked a flower."

"Button up. One tiny one is all I picked."

"Hi. What's in the jar?" Brian asked, coming up the porch steps.

"Daniel caught a butterfly and we're going to have babies," Joey started.

There goes the blabbermouth again, Daniel thought.

"Oh yeah?" Brian had something else on his mind. "Did you get a present for Eddie?" he asked after glancing in the jar. "I got a real neat telescope. It has a magnifying glass and compass attached and it all folds up. Great for camping out or detective and stuff. What are you getting?"

"Daniel's bringing two—Owww." Daniel brought his sneaker down hard on Joey's foot.

"Mom," Joey began.

"Cut it out," Daniel said, glaring at his brother. "I don't know yet," he told Brian. "I mean it's a surprise."

"Suit yourself. You guys want to play baseball?" Brian continued. "Everyone's down at Eddie's again. I don't think Tom will be there," he added, quickly.

"Ahh, not me," Daniel said. "I got stuff to do."

"What stuff?" Joey asked.

"None of your business."

"Hey, I will then," Joey said. "Just wait until I get my mitt."

Daniel watched his brother and Brian take off up the street. No way was he playing baseball again, all summer. Gets rid of Joey at least, he thought.

He looked back at the jar. The butterfly was beating its wings against the glass a mile a minute. Daniel could even hear it. A faint flicking sound. He couldn't stand it. This would never work. Its wings were sure to break. "Stop it," he shouted at the butterfly and shook the jar. "Stop it."

He could never keep a male and female in the same jar. It was too small. Slowly, Daniel unscrewed the lid and tilted the jar. The butterfly burst out and was gone over the porch roof. Daniel ran down the steps to watch it go. There just had to be some way to keep butterflies alive, he thought.

6

By Wednesday it was hotter than ever. Even the grass was brown and dry. It stuck into Daniel like little pins. He lay on his back and looked up at the clouds. Not a butterfly in sight. Everyone else was playing baseball again. It's too hot for baseball, Daniel thought. He got up and went into the house. In his room he changed shirts. His favorite shirt was stuffed back in his drawer where his mother couldn't find it. She was always putting things in the wash.

He felt the tab scrape his nose as he pulled the shirt over his head. Backwards. Daniel didn't care. The new shirt felt cool for a minute. It was his tie-dyed shirt. It reminded him of butterfly wings. He'd made it at camp last year. Only it was impossible to make anything as perfect as butterfly wings. He'd been drawing butterflies since first grade. He'd tried crayon, marker, paint, even chalk and glow-in-the-dark colors, and he still couldn't get it right. He was pretty good at it, though. Everyone else thought his pictures were great, even Eddie, and Eddie thought art was dumb. But Daniel knew they'd never be perfect.

Maybe Eddie would like a butterfly picture for his birthday. Framed. Nah, he couldn't bring a plain old picture. Maybe his tie-dyed shirt. Eddie liked it. He took a whiff under his arm. It smelled like dirty socks. He couldn't give Eddie a birthday gift that smelled like that. Daniel didn't want to think about it. He still had two days before the party, anyway.

Daniel went down to the basement. It was even hot in the basement. The drier was on. It smelled like wet clothes. Daniel looked around. Under the stairs he saw the cartons his mom had put there for recycling bottles and cans. One of them was overflowing. Pop cans were all over the floor. Daniel lifted a trash bag full of cans out of one of the cartons. He set it on the floor with a clatter.

In his father's tool room, Daniel found an old screen. He put some tape over the holes. He took some scissors and the box and screen and went outside.

His mother's garden didn't look so good. It was because of the drought, she had said. Maybe that's why there aren't so many butterflies, Daniel thought. He wondered if butterflies felt the heat.

Daniel threw some dirt into the bottom of the box. He pulled up some grass and threw it in. Then he snapped a few marigolds and petunias off their stems and put those in. He put the screen on top of the box. He picked up his net and waited.

By noontime all Daniel had were two cabbage whites, not even any sulphurs.

"Daniel," Joey called as he came around the side of the house on his bike. He jumped off the bike and threw it down all in one movement. He didn't even need the curb anymore. Daniel realized that Joey could really ride now.

"Want to practice catching with me?" Joey asked.

"Uh-uh," Daniel mumbled.

"Come on, Dan. We got to practice if we want to be good like—"

"Forget it," Daniel snapped. "It's too hot."

"Daniel," Joey tried again. "I was thinking, you're so fast when you catch butterflies. You're better than anyone. All you have to do is keep your eye on the ball, like catching a butterfly. That's what I do, and then—"

"I don't need baseball," Daniel interrupted.

Joey gave up. "Figure out what you're going to do about Eddie's present?"

"Don't remind me." Daniel sighed and laid his net down in the grass next to him. Butterflies never came when you waited for them.

Thump, thump, thump.

Joey was tossing a tennis ball against the garage and catching it with his glove.

"Cut that out," Daniel growled.

"Not hurting you."

"You'll scare the butterflies away."

"Hey, neat. Two butterflies. Can I see?"

"Don't touch that . . ."

Before Daniel had finished, Joey lifted the screen and two small white butterflies chased each other out of the box.

"Whiteys," Joey yelled. "Uh-oh," he added. "Sorry, Dan."

"They're cabbage whites," Daniel said as he jumped up with his net. "Now look what you did." The two butterflies were gone over the hedge. "I waited all morning for those two cabbage ones."

"I just wanted to see," Joey whined.

"Hey, Joey, want to play some baseball? We're meeting at Eddie's in five minutes," Brian said, coming down the driveway. Molly was waiting on the sidewalk.

Brian didn't even ask Daniel. Who cares, Daniel thought. He didn't really want to play, anyway. This way Joey would leave him alone.

Then Molly caught sight of Daniel's net. "Are you attacking those cute little butterflies again, Daniel King?" She rolled her bike closer. "I don't believe it! You're putting them in a cage. Daniel King, you're worse than those people Mrs. Reynolds told us about last year. The ones who steal dogs and keep them locked up in their own dirt. You are brutal," Molly called over her shoulder as she followed Joey and Brian down the driveway.

"Oh brother," Daniel mumbled to himself. He

kicked the box. Molly was right, he thought. This box was still too small. He needed something like an aviary, only for butterflies. A whole building where people could actually go inside. Something like the garage.

Daniel knew what he could do. Now he felt better. He always liked having a new project to work on. Who cared about baseball and Joey and Molly and dumb old birthday parties?

7

"That's final," Daniel's dad said the next day as he got into his car to go to work. "The garage is for a car."

Daniel looked around at the bicycles, bats, balls, a canoe, yard chairs, and garden tools that cluttered the garage. His dad was right. How could he keep butterflies in the garage? It was another dumb idea.

Daniel sat on the front steps and picked at the callus on the bottom of his foot.

"Daniel, put your shoes on if you leave the yard," his mother called through the screen door. "With socks," she added.

Daniel liked going barefoot. Shoes made his feet sweat. And the thought of putting clean socks on his dry feet made shivers run up his spine. He always saved a used pair of socks under his bed for when his mom made him wear socks. Daniel's dad had told him that in some parts of the world people went barefoot all their lives. The bottoms of their feet got so tough, they didn't need shoes. Daniel thought that was neat. He thought maybe he could try that. Maybe if his feet got real tough he could try going barefoot in the snow.

A large delivery truck pulled up in front of Daniel's house. For a minute, Daniel felt excited. Something was going to happen. Then the truck backed up to Mrs. Berger's house and stopped. Two men got out and unloaded a box. It was big, the kind of box that was good for puppet stages or forts. The men carried the box up to Mrs. Berger's front door. They opened one end and slid a refrigerator out. They strapped the refrigerator to a kind of cart with wheels. Mrs. Berger opened the door and the men lifted the loaded cart up the steps. Must be heavy, Daniel thought.

He looked at the box. It had the word *Whirl-pool* written on the side. There was a design made of slanted circles. It was neat the way a few lines like that could look as if they were moving. Daniel had tried to make his butterfly drawings look as if they were moving.

Suddenly, Daniel had an idea. "Perfect," he whispered to himself. He jumped up and ran over to Mrs. Berger's house.

He ran up the steps and rang the bell. "Can I have the box?" he asked when Mrs. Berger came to the door.

"I don't see why not." She smiled. "Saves me getting rid of it." Daniel thanked her and started dragging the box over to his driveway. It was heavy. There were wooden blocks in the bottom. Daniel took them out. Then he crawled inside.

This was just what he needed. It would be better to keep the box sideways. He couldn't stand up in it, but there was more room and he could easily sit in it. He made plans. A screen on one end for light and air. A door in the middle. Great.

"Hey, neat, a fort." It was Joey. Thump. The

43

box shook. That kid had kicked it. Daniel kept quiet. Maybe Joey wouldn't know he was inside and he'd go away.

"I know you're in there, Dan," Joey called.

Daniel couldn't believe it. Just when he had the perfect project, Joey had to start bothering him. He was always hanging around when Daniel wanted to be alone.

Daniel thought about Brian. Next week, Brian was going to stay with his father for a long time, four whole weeks. Daniel wished his dad lived far away so he could go visit him without Joey. Daniel wondered what it would be like if his parents lived apart, the way Brian's did. Then he could live with one and Joey could live with the other. He wondered which one he would choose to live with. He couldn't decide. He felt bad. Maybe it was better to live together, even if it meant living with Joey. Maybe they could send Joey away for a while, to camp or something.

Thump. Joey kicked the box again. Daniel couldn't stand it. "Cut that out."

"I knew you were in there," Joey said. "We can make a great fort."

"It's not a fort," Daniel yelled, "and it's not we, it's me."

"Mo-o-om." Daniel could see through the open flap that Joey had started toward the house. "Daniel won't let me play with the box."

Mom came to the back door. "Joey, why don't you help me make lunch, then we can bake brownies for dessert."

"Oh boy, I get to lick the bowl," Joey said. He stuck his chin out and stared at Daniel through the open end of the box.

As if I care, Daniel thought as Joey ran into the house. Daniel lay back in his box and stretched out. His mom was OK. She sure knew how to handle Joey all right. And his box was perfect for the butterfly barn.

It was cooler in the box. Maybe he'd just stay there with the butterflies. Like being in his own cocoon. If he could just forget that Eddie's party was that afternoon and he still didn't have a decent present, and if he didn't ever have to hear about baseball again, things would be OK.

8

Daniel sat in his butterfly barn after lunch. He already had two cabbage butterflies and a swallowtail. I'd like an admiral to add to my exhibit, he thought.

Daniel had put bottle caps with sugar water in them in the box for his butterflies to drink. But they didn't seem to be taking any. He dipped his finger in one of the caps. It was sticky. He thought about taking a lick himself. Instead he slowly moved his finger toward the swallowtail clinging to the flower stem at the corner of the box.

"Come on," Daniel coaxed, "take a taste." He

waited very quiet and still. The butterfly fluttered its wings. Daniel held his breath. The next thing he knew, she had landed on his finger. Her legs tickled, pricked, almost. Daniel couldn't believe it. He was actually feeding a swallowtail from his own finger. He was probably the first kid ever to do it. He was so excited, he wanted to pet the butterfly. He wanted to hold it.

Slowly, Daniel raised his free hand. Gently, he put his fingers on her wings. That startled the butterfly and Daniel let go. "I shouldn't have done that," he muttered. He looked at his fingers. There was an almost perfect print of the butterfly design on his fingers in yellow and black and gold. It was beautiful.

"Hey, Daniel, you in there?" That was Brian's voice.

Daniel stuck his head out the door. "Yep."

"What're you doing?"

"Feeding my butterflies."

"Hey." Molly was there too. She stuck her face up to the screen at the end of the box. She was wearing a baseball cap, backward. Thinks she's cool, Daniel thought.

"He's got butterflies in there," Molly said.

"Can I come in?" Brian asked. He opened the

door wider. The box shook as the door scraped across the driveway.

"Sure," Daniel said. "Take it easy, though."

Brian shut the door and sat back on his heels. "Neat."

They could hear Molly walking around outside.

"Watch," Daniel said. He showed Brian how to dip his finger in the sugar water.

As he moved his finger toward the swallowtail, Molly knocked on the box. "Don't you touch that poor insect."

The butterfly flew to the other end of the box.

"I wasn't touching him. You scared him," Daniel yelled.

"Well, I'm not hanging around to watch you torture butterflies. See you at Eddie's," she called.

Brian raised his eyebrows. Then he started to crawl out of the box. "Joey's making brownies. We need another player. Want to play some ball?"

"I don't think so," Daniel said. "I've got to feed my butterflies."

Brian shrugged. "You're coming to Eddie's party, aren't you?"

"Sure," Daniel said. "See you then."

"The party," he said to himself. It was in a couple of hours. He hoped Molly wouldn't be there.

Suddenly he heard a horrible sound from the kitchen. It was a cry and a scream all at once. It got louder. Daniel's heart began to pound. It sounded like Joey but it didn't. The noise stopped, then it started again, louder.

Daniel heard Mom's voice. "Joey," she screamed.

Daniel scrambled to get out of the box. He stumbled out the door opening and then raced to the back door. Joey was always crying or yelling about something, but this was different. Daniel knew it.

He reached for the door and ran inside. There was Joey standing on a chair by the stove. His eyes were wide and his face was white. He held his right hand up and looked at it and started to scream again, an awful scream. No tears, but his mouth stretched into a terrible shape.

Mom picked Joey up in her arms. "Don't look at it," she said, carrying him to the sink. Then she saw Daniel. "Hold your brother," she said. "He burned his hand. He leaned his full weight on it on the burner when he reached for the spatula. I don't know why it was on high," she said, desperately. Then, in her take-charge voice again, she said, "Keep his hand in the water." She turned off the tap and went to the phone.

Daniel saw the red hot coils of the large burner. Like lava. It was still on. Quickly he flipped the knob and turned the stove off. Then he felt helpless. Joey was whimpering now. Daniel went over to his brother at the sink and began patting him lightly on the back. He looked at the floor. Then he glanced up under his lashes to look at Joey's hand. He didn't want to but he had to. It looked awful. There were blisters all over it. One in each little section and in lines all across his little palm. It made the design of the rings of the stove. Something smelled burned. Daniel kept looking at it. Then he felt sick. He remembered how much one tiny little blister had burned when he had touched the hot iron once. It had hurt all day.

Joey started to cry, real tears now. He looked at his hand and screamed again. He tried to grab it.

"Don't touch it," Daniel yelled. "Keep it in the water." He caught Joey by the wrist of the burned hand and held it firmly. Gently, he dipped the hand into the sink. He put his other arm around his brother and held him tightly.

"Don't look at it, Joey," he said more gently. Then he hugged Joey more tightly. He wanted to make the scream stop with his body.

Joey was shaking. "It hurts, it hurts, it hurts," he kept saying. Daniel wished Mom would hurry.

"Mom's calling the doctor," Daniel said softly. "It'll be OK. They'll make it stop." He just kept talking, saying anything that came into his head. He didn't know if he was talking to Joey or himself. He was rocking a bit. They both stood there rocking and Daniel kept talking. And then Daniel noticed that Joey was beginning to quiet down.

"It will be OK, Joey." Mom picked Joey up. "Thanks, Daniel." Joey started to cry louder again. "I have to take Joey to the emergency room," Mom said. "The doctor thinks it's probably a second-degree burn, but he's concerned because it's on the hand and he wants to be sure. I called your father. He's going to meet us at the hospital." She rushed around the house collecting her purse and keys. "Listen, Daniel, I didn't

get to wrap Eddie's gift yet. It's on my bed with the wrapping paper. You can get the scissors and tape and do it. Watch your time. It's nearly two o'clock now."

"But, Mom." Daniel followed his mother and brother to the door. "Can't I go too? I don't care about Eddie's old party."

"Daniel, this may take a long time, and it works out well that you have someplace to go. I'll call from the hospital and let Eddie's mother know. You can stay there until we get home." Then she bent over and kissed Daniel on the head. Joey was still crying. "Don't worry," she told Daniel, but her smile was shaky.

9

It seemed extra quiet without Joey's screaming. Too quiet. Daniel thought about what he knew about burns. He wondered if they would have to take skin off another part of Joey's body, a flat part like his leg, and put it on his hand. The idea gave him shivers. He didn't want to think about it. Poor Joey. He wouldn't be able to go swimming. Once, when Brian got his finger caught in a door, he had four stitches and couldn't go swimming for two weeks. Daniel figured a burn was worse than stitches. And it was Joey's right hand. He wouldn't be able to catch butterflies anymore. Daniel wished now he had let him help with the butterfly barn. And what about baseball? Daniel remembered. Joey wouldn't be able to catch or bat, and he really loved baseball. He was good at it too. Suddenly, Daniel didn't feel like being alone.

He went to the bedroom and quickly wrapped the two books for Eddie. He slapped one long piece of tape over the whole package. Then he scribbled a card with Eddie's name on it. He made a quick butterfly design too, and taped the card to the present.

At the party everyone wanted to hear about Joey. Daniel told them about the blisters on every section of Joey's palm.

"Daniel, you are disgusting," said Molly.

"Come on, Molly. He's just telling what happened," Brian said. "Maybe your dad could arrest him." He stuck an elbow in Daniel's side and they both laughed.

"Hey," Molly said. "Joey won't be able to play ball. Who's going to play second base for us?"

Before they could decide, Eddie's mom began to organize the games. The whole party was about baseball. Everyone got a baseball cap and trading cards for favors. Boy, Eddie sure had baseball on the brain, Daniel thought.

They played baseball trivia. Daniel didn't know any of the answers. Joey would know, though, he thought. Daniel started to worry about Joey again. When the game was over, he asked Eddie's mom if he could call the hospital. She told Daniel not to worry, his mother would call as soon as she could. But Daniel still felt worried.

Finally, Eddie's mother said, "Time for cake. And then we'll open the presents."

Presents. Daniel remembered. He looked at the pile of gifts on the coffee table. How could he have forgotten? There, wrapped in blue paper with colored balloons all over it, were the books he was giving Eddie. He had been so worried about Joey, Daniel had forgotten to think about his gift and how everyone was going to laugh. For almost two whole hours, all Daniel had done was think about Joey.

Everyone else went into the dining room. Daniel went over to the pile of gifts. Anyone could tell his gift was books. He should have disguised them. Put them in a shoe box or something. Why couldn't his mom have at least picked a book about baseball? Maybe she hated baseball as much as he did. Daniel picked up the package and slid it under the pile of presents. There. Maybe Eddie would forget about it. Maybe everyone would have to leave before he got to open it. Maybe the card would fall off and no one would know who it was from. Maybe I should just leave, Daniel thought. But he knew he couldn't do that.

He went into the dining room. Everyone else was sitting at the table. The cake looked like a baseball diamond. It had little plastic players on it. Everyone got to choose one. It was a chocolate cake with green icing for grass.

Daniel couldn't eat his piece of cake. It made him think of Joey. And when everyone finished eating cake, Eddie would open the presents. Everyone would know what a dumb present he had brought. He'd probably never get invited to another party.

Daniel watched Brian stuff a huge chunk of cake into his mouth. "Do you have to eat like that?" he asked.

Cake crumbs trickled down Brian's shirt. He couldn't answer with a full mouth. He crossed his eyes and almost choked trying to swallow the cake.

"Forget it," Daniel told him.

Eddie picked up the knife and lopped off another piece of cake for himself. "Hey," he said, contemplating his handiwork. "You think they'll have to amputate Joey's hand?"

"Eddie, that's disgusting," Molly yelled.

"Cut it out," Daniel said.

"Just kidding," Eddie said.

"I'll wrap your cake," Eddie's mom told Daniel. "You can take it home."

I'll give it to Joey, Daniel thought. Maybe Eddie was right. What if they did have to amputate? What would Joey do with only one hand? His left hand. He wouldn't be able to eat cake.

There weren't many things you could do with one hand. Read books, maybe. *Books.* Daniel remembered. Eddie was about to open the presents, and this was about to become his last birthday party ever.

10

There were only two presents left to open. Daniel could see the corner of his flat, skinny little package under all the discarded wrapping paper and bows. The card was barely hanging on with a twisted piece of tape.

The phone rang. Eddie's mom went to answer it. Eddie reached for the other present. He tore the paper off. It was Brian's telescope.

"Hey, this is neat. It'll be great to take camping. Thanks, Brian."

Everyone tried out the magnifying glass. They wanted to know where Brian had gotten it.

"Daniel," Eddie's mom said. "That was your

mother on the phone. She said to tell you they are home. Everything is OK and you can go home anytime."

Saved by the bell, Daniel thought. This was his chance. He had a great excuse to escape before Eddie got to his present.

"Hey look," said Brian. "One more present. It almost got lost in the trash. Open it, Eddie."

Too late. Some best friend Brian was.

"It must be Daniel's," Molly said. "He's the only one left."

Leave it to Molly to keep count, Daniel thought.

"Books," said Eddie. "I can tell." By then the paper was off.

"What are they?" Everyone strained to see.

"Mom, look." Eddie held up one book. "Daniel gave me a butterfly guide."

"We can take it on vacation," his mom said.

Mothers always liked books, Daniel thought.

"Yeah," Eddie said. "We see millions of butterflies when we go camping."

"Oh," Brian said, "this is a great book. I read it this year." He held up the mystery book.

"You'll like it, Eddie," Molly said. "It's weird, but it's just your speed."

Daniel hadn't known Molly ever read books. He thought all she cared about was baseball. And Brian had never mentioned that he'd read the book. It was one of Daniel's favorites. He had read it twice.

Everyone was discussing their favorite part.

"Don't tell me the ending," Eddie reminded them.

"Daniel," Brian asked, "have you read the next book in the series? I have it, if you want to borrow it."

"Sure," Daniel said.

How come I never discussed books with these guys before, he wondered. It was great to know they liked to read too . . . something besides baseball. Maybe they had some other books to share. Daniel felt really good for the first time since Joey got burned. Suddenly he wanted to be home. He wanted to tell his mom how the kids liked his present. He wanted to see Joey, and he wanted to sit inside his butterfly barn and think or read. It would be a great place to read.

"See you after dinner," Eddie yelled as everyone was leaving the party. "My backyard. Bring your gloves."

"Hey, Daniel, we could use another player,"

Brian suggested as he and Molly walked home with Daniel. "Can you play ball after dinner?"

Molly agreed. "You could take Joey's place. Well, not exactly take his place. Someone could come in from the outfield, and I'll cover first, but . . ."

"Knock it off, Molly," Brian cut her short. "We need all the kids we can get."

"Right," she said. "See you later." Molly turned down her street.

Brian lowered his voice. "Tom's gone to camp. He's away for four weeks."

Daniel figured Brian was a real friend. He knew just how Daniel felt about Tom. It was nice to know Tom was gone, but Tom was only half the problem. Daniel was a lousy baseball player. He was afraid of the ball, and he could never begin to replace Joey.

Even so, Daniel felt excited. He'd found out something new about his friends. They liked to read just like he did, and they liked some of the same books. Maybe his summer wasn't lost.

"I'll see," he told Brian. "I've got to check on Joey now."

"Yeah," Brian agreed. "See you later." He nodded as he turned down his own walk.

11

"Hey, Daniel. Look what I got." Joey was waving a can of soda and a bag of cheese snacks in Daniel's face. Their mom only allowed soda on special occasions, and she almost never allowed cheese snacks. These were the kind that made your fingers orange.

"And look at my hand." Joey held up a huge white abominable-snowman hand. It had orange cheese specks on it, and it was already getting dirty.

"Hi, Daniel," their father said over the top of the newspaper. "Looks like a mummy's hand. The great white monster from the tomb." He laughed.

Daniel was barely in the door and he could see that Joey was getting even more attention than usual. Everyone was pretty relaxed and happy, and Daniel figured that meant Joey probably wasn't about to lose his hand. Joey was climbing all over the back of the couch, and no one even stopped him. Here Daniel had been worried all afternoon, and now everyone was joking and eating cheese snacks.

"Daniel, guess what? We're having pizza tonight. My choice, pepperoni."

Figures, Daniel thought, since mushroom was his favorite. His mood had changed in an instant, even though pizza was his favorite meal. "Big deal," he said to Joey. "Hey, Mom, where's *my* soda?"

"We didn't get you one." Joey smiled as if that was good news. "Want a sip?" He stuck a can of root beer toward Daniel. It had little orange cheese-snack crumbs all around the hole.

"No way. Not with your germs. You're pretty tough stuff for someone who was such a crybaby a little while ago," Daniel said. "Too bad you don't have a real cast, so kids could write all over it." Daniel had always thought it would be neat to have a cast. Nothing big, a broken ankle or wrist or something. Now he felt like being mean. He almost wished he had a burned hand.

"Mom," Joey called, beginning to sulk. He slid down the back of the couch to a sitting position. "Daniel's being mean." Then he perked up again. "Look what else I got. A baseball book. At the hospital gift shop. We got something for you, too, but I'm not giving it to you."

Mom came into the room. "Settle down, boys. Daniel, I expect some help from you. Joey's hand is going to be all right. But it has to stay bandaged so it will heal. He can't be too rough, and he has to keep it clean and dry. Now that means no swimming, and there are some things he'll need help with for a while, like buttons and zippers." She gave Daniel a hug. "I know I can count on you."

Daniel felt sulky. He knew he shouldn't have teased Joey. He wanted everyone to be happy again, so he said, "OK, Mom." Then he gave her a silly grin. "Now, how about my surprise?"

"Oh, it's just something little. Joey picked it out. He'll give it to you."

Joey was struggling with a bag, trying to hold it open and take something out at the same time. He even tried using his teeth.

"Here," he said finally, holding a book up for Daniel. "It's all about butterflies. *How to A-ttr-act Butterflies.* I got it because I thought maybe it meant how to trap them with a kind of mousetrap or something. You know, only with a net that slaps down on them when they try to get the food."

Daniel got shivers at the thought of a mousetrap slapping closed on a butterfly, or even a mouse for that matter. Molly would have a fit.

"Thanks," Daniel said. "This looks great." The book reminded Daniel about his butterfly barn. He hadn't checked it all afternoon.

"I'm not going to be much good at helping to catch butterflies," Joey said. "I can't even look at this dumb old baseball book with one hand." It was a paperback and the pages were stiff. Daniel could see they kept flipping. Joey needed one hand to hold the book and the fingers of his other hand to turn the pages. Poor Joey didn't have an amputation, but he was going to have a rough time for a while. Then Daniel remembered something.

"Eddie's mom sent you a birthday bag. Take a look at this. I'll help you with your book later."

Daniel dumped the bag out so Joey could see everything. "I have to go check on something," he told Joey.

Before he even got out the back door, Daniel could see his butterfly barn in the middle of the driveway where he had left it. And he could see the door stuck open, just the way he had left it when he had run into the house after Joey got burned. He stooped down and crawled inside the box. It was empty except for a few twigs and wilted leaves and flowers and bottle caps with dried-up sugar water. Daniel punched the side of the box. None of his plans ever worked.

It's my own stupid fault, Daniel thought. He wanted to blame someone else, like Joey for getting burned, or his mom for asking him to hold Joey, or for that matter both his parents for even having a second kid in the family. But he knew he couldn't. He had left the door open himself.

He looked around at the wilted leaves. The box felt hot and stuffy. Those butterflies couldn't live in here anyway, he thought. It's too hot. It was just another dumb idea.

Daniel looked at the book in his hand. What

good was a book about attracting butterflies if you couldn't keep them, anyway? He might as well give up.

He leaned back against the side of the box and flipped through the pages. There were some interesting drawings. Maybe he'd have to stick to drawing butterflies. Or, maybe he should forget about butterflies altogether.

One chapter was called "Butterfly Gardens." Daniel immediately thought of butterflies growing on stems, all colors and sizes. You could pick them. He could draw a picture of that.

He stretched out to read. Joey was right about one thing. If he couldn't have a butterfly barn, this box made a great fort.

12

Daniel sat on the front porch after supper. He watched Mr. Ivy across the street cut the lawn with his old hand mower. It made a nice clicking sound. Daniel could smell the grass. This was the best time of the day. Everyone slowed down. It was cooler. Already some moms and dads were sitting out on the porches, joking and laughing. And there was still time to play. Daniel felt pretty good too.

Even the pepperoni pizza had tasted good. He'd eaten five pieces. Of course he took the pepperoni off first. He made a tower with the little round slices. By the time he had finished dinner he had at least a two-inch tower of pepperoni.

Now Daniel had plans to make. He liked making plans. Daniel figured he felt best when he had a new idea, like now.

"Hey, Dan, look, two admirals. Right there. I'll get the nets. No, I can't. You get the nets. I'll watch them." Joey was jumping up and down all over the place. "Or I can get the nets. You just catch them. Come on, Dan. There's two."

Daniel laughed. Joey was pretty funny when he got excited. He watched the two butterflies chase each other as if they were playing. The way he and Joey did. He wondered if butterflies did that. Play. He wondered if butterflies fought, too. Probably not. They were too smart for that. Too beautiful. Maybe they were mating or something. Daniel watched their movements, quick and smooth at the same time. And the colors. A miracle. That was the only way to describe it. No one could have thought of making butterflies if they didn't already exist.

Joey was back with the nets. "Daniel," he almost screamed, "they'll get away!"

"It's OK," Daniel said. "I'm not catching any more butterflies."

"You mean never?" Joey's hand, outstretched with the nets, dropped to his side. His shoulders slumped. "I thought you needed more for your barn. And what about your collection?"

"I'm finished with the barn. You were right. The box makes a better fort."

"Daniel!" Joey screamed. "You can't just give up!" He was red in the face. "Just because a few butterflies got away! I'll catch them with my left hand. Just watch!" Joey took off down the steps.

Daniel watched him. One thing about Joey, he sure didn't give up. He worked hard on things he cared about. Daniel could see why everyone liked his brother. And right now Joey was really worried about Daniel and his butterflies, just as Daniel had worried about Joey's hand. He really was a great little kid.

Joey made a few useless swipes with the net and then watched as the two admirals escaped over Mr. Ivy's roof. Daniel could see there was no way Joey was going to catch butterflies with his left hand without a lot more practice.

Joey walked slowly back to the steps with his head down. "Gone," he said, sitting down next to Daniel on the top step. "You could have had them. One anyway." A big tear rolled down his

73

cheek. "Aren't you ever going to catch any more butterflies? I can't with this dumb old bandage. I have to wear it for two weeks or more. Maybe forever. What if my fingers don't work or something when it comes off? Then I'll never be able to do anything good again." Joey was really crying now.

Daniel patted Joey on the shoulder. "Your fingers will be fine in a few weeks. The doctor said so."

"But what about the butterflies? You're so smart and you know so much about them, you can't just stop like that. I told all my friends in school about your collection and how I help you and everything."

Daniel was quiet for a minute. He hadn't known that Joey really cared about his projects. He had thought all the little guy wanted to do was make trouble.

"Listen, Joey," he said. "I have a better idea, and I got it from that book you brought home for me. I'm going to make a butterfly garden, and you can help. Mom says we can use the flower bed on Mrs. Berger's side of the house. That book tells exactly what to plant to attract what kind of butterflies. That way we can keep the butterflies alive and still see them. We can make pictures, photographs, maybe. The book even tells how to get them to reproduce. It'll be like a butterfly preserve."

"Can I really help?" Joey asked, wiping his face with his left hand.

"Sure," Daniel said. "I bet even Molly will like the idea. Maybe some of the other kids will help too. Eddie really liked the butterfly book I gave him for his birthday."

Joey looked at his bandaged hand. "I bet all those guys are playing ball right now without me. No one even came to ask if I could play. All I can do now is watch all summer. Baseball is the only thing I'm good at. Dad says I'm a natural. Not anymore." Joey sounded as if he was going to cry again.

"I've been thinking about that too," Daniel said. "Wait here. I'll be right back." Daniel ran into the house and came back with his glove. "Let's go, Joey," he said. "We can start right now. I bet those guys will still be playing for another half hour or so. We can't take the bikes, with your hand. We'll have to walk, so hurry."

"I don't want to go," Joey whined. "You know I can't play."

"Trust me," Daniel said. "Those guys need you."

Joey dragged himself off the front steps and slowly followed Daniel up the street. "Come on," Daniel coaxed him. "Before it gets too dark."

When they got to Eddie's yard, everyone crowded around Joey. They all wanted to know how he was and how his hand felt.

Daniel stood back while Joey told the whole story. He didn't even feel jealous. He felt good for Joey that everyone wanted to see him.

Finally Molly said, "Too bad you can't play, Joey."

Then Daniel spoke up. "That's why we're here. Joey's going to play."

"Come on, Dan, you know I can't," Joey said.

"I don't think he's much of a lefty," Brian said.

"I'll be Joey's hands," Daniel explained. "I'll bat and catch and Joey can run. And," he added, "we count as a whole out. No half outs." Daniel put his arm around Joey's shoulders. Joey was grinning. "Joey and me together."

"That's a great idea," Brian said.

"We really need players," Eddie agreed.

"Joey can run fast enough for two players," Molly said. "It's worth a try."

Daniel was happy the kids liked his idea, but he was nervous. Maybe the kids just felt bad for Joey, or maybe they thought Daniel really had a chance now he and Joey were a team. They hadn't even put him at the end of the batting order. His team was up and he was up second. All he had to do now was hit the ball.

Joey got ready to run. He was standing to the side, a little behind Daniel. Daniel stood up at home plate. He checked to make sure he wouldn't hit Joey and swung the bat a few times. Then he waited for the pitch.

Brian wound up and threw the ball. He did it so smoothly, Daniel thought. Natural. Daniel swung. Strike. He was too late. His hands were sweaty. He wiped them on his pants. "Keep your eye on the ball," Joey had said, "like chasing butterflies."

Brian threw the ball again. Crack!

Daniel felt his bat connect with the ball, a clean smooth hit. It felt good. It felt great. Daniel almost started to run to first himself. Everyone was cheering. Daniel watched Joey pass first

base. Boy, he was fast. He just made it to second and stopped before Brian could tag him.

Joey was jumping up and down. "You did it, Daniel! A double on the first hit."

"We did it together," Daniel yelled.

"Not bad," Brian called from the pitcher's mound.

"This will work great," Molly agreed.

"Yeah," Daniel said. "It's OK." He stood behind home plate with his teammates. Molly was up.

Maybe this summer was going to be OK after all. He had a new butterfly project, one that he knew was going to work. He had some books he couldn't wait to trade with Brian and Eddie, maybe even Molly. And he could play a little baseball. This summer was going to be OK. It was going to be the best.